D1147965

WALKER BOOKS

For my family and my beloved husband
O.M.

For my mum and dad
S.H.

First published 2021 by Walker Books Ltd
87 Vauxhall Walk, London SE11 5HJ

2 4 6 8 10 9 7 5 3 1

Text © 2021 Oti Mabuse
Illustrations © 2021 Samara Hardy
The Bird Jive Song © 2021 Thomas Sutcliffe

This book has been typeset in DIN Schrift and WB Samara

Printed in Italy

British Library Cataloguing in Publication Data: a catalogue
record for this book is available from the British Library

ISBN 978-1-4063-9996-7

www.walker.co.uk

WALKER BOOKS
AND SUBSIDIARIES

LONDON • BOSTON • SYDNEY • AUCKLAND

DANCE WITH OTi

THE
Bird Jive

Oti Mabuse

ILLUSTRATED BY
Samara Hardy

It was the first day of dance class.
All the children lined up outside
Mrs Oti's dance studio.

Mrs Oti was so excited to meet the children and teach them their very first dance steps.

"Welcome, everyone! We're going to have lots of fun!" she said.

"Before we start dancing, let's warm up and stretch," said Mrs Oti. "Here we go!"

WARM UP

1 Jump up and down as if you're skipping rope.

2 Do ten jumping jacks!

3 Lunge from side to side.

4 Stretch your right hand over!

5 Stretch your left hand over!

"OK! Now it's time to learn our first dance. It's called the jive," said Mrs Oti.

Both hands UP.

Both hands DOWN.

Jump to the LEFT.

Jump to the RIGHT.

Ooops! Fikile was so busy looking at her sparkly new dance shoes, she missed the first steps! "Don't worry, Fikile." Mrs Oti smiled. "Let's try again."

The class jumped to the left but Gan forgot which way to go.

"Follow me," said Martin.

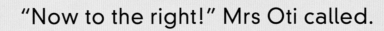

"Now to the right!" Mrs Oti called.

"Perfect. Great teamwork, boys!" said Mrs Oti.

"OK, let's learn the next part of our dance," Mrs Oti said.

Clap RIGHT. Clap LEFT. Then Kick, Kick, Kick!

Poor Poppy couldn't keep up!

"Don't be upset, little one," said Mrs Oti. "Close your eyes and listen to the music."

Poppy took a deep breath and began to dance to the beat.

"That's right, Poppy! Feel the rhythm," said Mrs Oti.

"OK, children, we're halfway through. Now for the tricky bit," called Mrs Oti.

Two twists ...

and four twists ...

WIGGLE THOSE HANDS!

Theo twisted and twisted the best he could.

"You go, Theo!" said Mrs Oti. "That's the way!"

All of a sudden ... a beautiful green bird flew into the room!
It flapped and flapped around the dance studio.

"Don't worry children, I've got this!" Mrs Oti said, opening the window.

SQUAWK!!

"Ooooooh!" Naira pointed. She had never been so close to a bird before.

"Bye-bye, birdie!" called Mrs Oti.

"But wait … that bird has given me an idea!

Everyone grab a feather from the dressing up box."

The children laughed as
Mrs Oti began flapping her arms.

Flap those hands
UP and DOWN.

The children squawked, hopped and flapped their arms just like the little bird.

Mrs Oti clapped her hands over the noise.
"Time to learn our next move," she laughed.

Roll your hips ROUND and ROUND ...

and slide to the LEFT.

Then the class heard a massive
THUMP. Olivia had slipped and
fallen on the floor.

"Up you get, Olivia! Style
it out and make it look
cool!" said Mrs Oti.

Theo helped Olivia up.
"That's my special dance
move," Olivia laughed.

"Great work, Olivia! Now, all of you..."

Two twists ...

and four twists ...

WIGGLE THOSE HANDS!

"Now for the last steps of the day. Here we go!"

Slide to the RIGHT ...

Kick to the LEFT ...

Kick to the RIGHT and ...

POSE!

"Well done, class!
I'm so proud of you all."
Mrs Oti smiled.

"Shall we perform our
dance for everyone?"
she asked, as the families
came in to watch.

"Are you ready? Let's do
THE BIRD JIVE!"

Everyone clapped and cheered as the dance ended.

"Look!" Mrs Oti pointed at the window. "You were so good – even the birds came back to watch."

The children laughed
and gave a little bow.

"See you next week!"
they waved.

THE BIRD JIVE: STEP BY STEP

1 Both hands UP.
Both hands DOWN.

2 Jump to the LEFT.
Jump to the RIGHT.

3 Clap RIGHT. Clap LEFT.
Kick, Kick, Kick!

6 Roll your hips
ROUND and ROUND.

7 Slide to the LEFT.

8 Two twists.
Four twists.

4 Two twists.
Four twists.

5 Flap those hands
UP and DOWN.

9 Slide to the RIGHT.

10 Kick to the LEFT.
Kick to the RIGHT.

And ... POSE!

About Mrs Oti

Oti Mabuse is a world championship dancer and choreographer, best-known for her star quality on BBC's Number One show "Strictly Come Dancing" and CBeebies' "Boogie Beebies".

Oti was born in South Africa and has been dancing since she was four years old. She's one of the most successful South African dancers in the world – and is also a trained civil engineer, which makes her super-talented!

About the jive

The jive is a dance created by African Americans in the early 1930s in the USA. It became popular all over the world with its fast rhythm and catchy beat! Today, the jive is one of five international Latin dances in competition.

Watch a step-by-step tutorial and listen to "The Bird Jive" song by pointing the camera on your smartphone at the QR code below!

dance-with-oti.walker.co.uk